This Book Belongs to

Grace ♡

who is a good friend of Peter and Percy.

WOR PETER AND WOR PERCY

This FIRST EDITION is published *by*
DIZZY B PRODUCTIONS
peterandpercy@gmail.com

ISBN 978-1-9996595-3-0

Illustration Copyright © 2018 *by* LIZZIE CARINS
Story Copyright © 2018 *by* D. B. COURT

Story *by* D. B. COURT
Illustrations *by* LIZZIE CARINS
Story Research *by* RICHARD M. TOLSON
Designed *by* DANNY NANOS

Printed in *the* UNITED KINGDOM

Thanks to our generous sponsors:

HOLBRIX LTD. • ALTORIA DEVELOPMENT LTD. • LORD RIDLEY

Wor Peter and Wor Percy & The Great War Adventure

A cowardly cat's search for courage.

Story by D. B. COURT • Illustrations by LIZZIE CARINS
Story Research by RICHARD M. TOLSON

CHAPTER 1

A Cat Stuck On A Rock

RIDLEY FLEXED HIS FRONT LEGS AND PULLED IN HIS BELLY, before checking the shape of his shadow. It looked more like a soggy sack of potatoes than a cat. That's what came of too many lazy days doing nothing. But at least sitting up on his rock kept him safe and out of harm's way. He gave his fur a lick and tried not to think of the old days, when he'd been like a mighty lion. Back then, all the creatures on Lord Ridley's Blagdon Estate had feared him, admired him and kept a respectful distance. But that was before the arrival of Archie-the-Fiend. Now everyone knew that Ridley spent his days cowering up on his rock, a cowardly cat, twitching with fear when he so much as glimpsed a ripple of movement in the long grass.

Ridley's stomach did a low growl. It had been a whole day since his last meal, but until Percy turned up to tell him the coast was clear of the Fiend, there was no way he could go hunting. Too risky.

At last he saw a flash of chestnut. In his usual way Percy leapt high over the black-thorn hedge. But then, as the stallion galloped across the field, his long tail whipped at the air as if monsters were chasing after him. Something was up. Ridley knew it. Spitting out a stray piece of moss, he paced back and forth on his rock scanning the horizon. No sign of the vicious fur ball anywhere, and surely even a cat as mean as The Fiend would think twice about attacking a stallion? There must be some other monster on the loose.

Percy whinnied. "I've been chosen! I've been chosen!" he yelled as he charged across the last stretch of grass, and then skidded to a halt in front of Ridley's rock.

"Chosen for what?" Ridley purred, "Has Jasper Ridley decided to ride you in the Ridley Christmas Race?"

"No! No! Something even better than that. I can't believe it! I've been chosen to go on a Great Adventure," Percy said, baring his teeth in a horsey grin.

Ridley's left eye gave an involuntary twitch. "An adventure? I don't like the sound of that!" he mumbled.

"This morning a man came to the stable. Out of all the horses, he chose me. Me! A very fine looking man he was too, one of the Northumberland Hussars. Off we went together, trotting through the streets of Newcastle on a grand parade. Isn't that marvellous! That's why I'm so late. And look, he's engraved his initials - see - here on my right hoof: HBR. Harold Burge Robson! What do you think to that?"

"It sounds like a bubbling cauldron of trouble to me."

"Don't be such a scaredy cat. And - well - there's another bit of news. I don't know how to tell you this, so I'd best tell you quickly. We're off tomorrow, Harold and I!"

All the hairs on Ridley's body stood up as if a bolt of lightning had shot through both of his ears. "Off? What ... where ... what do you mean, *off*?" he said, and swallowed hard.

"I can't go on a great adventure without leaving home. You, of all cats, should know that, what with all the adventures you used to go on," Percy said, swinging his head a little too wildly so that his mane gave Ridley's nose a sharp whip. "Sorry," he said.

But Ridley didn't notice the sting of horse hair. He was too busy worrying about his tongue. It had turned all dry and salty and he could no longer swallow. "But ... but ...!" He tried to spit out more words, but now his tongue had tied in a knot. So he tried again, "but ... who ... who will p... protect me from the *FIEND*?"

"Ah. Him. Come on Ridley, you have to stop worrying about the Fiend."

"Stop worrying about the worst sort of tom cat in the world, a greedy bully? Never satisfied sticking to his own territory, oh no! He has to stomp all over the homes of every cat in the world, causing pain and destruction wherever he goes!"

"I see your point," said Percy. "But I remember a time when you would have seen him off with a bite to his bum and a flea in his ear!"

"That was then. This is now!" Ridley muttered as he dabbed his damaged left eye with his paw. He remembered then only too well. When a small cat had started strolling through his fields Ridley had thought nothing of it. They'd come face to face once or twice.

"Hello, I'm Archie," the cat had purred.

Except for the mop of long black hair swept across the top of his head, and the curious black tuft under his nose, his mottled coat looked thin and shabby. Ridley remembered thinking that this cat looked weak and weedy, not enemy material at all. That was his mistake. It turned out Archie was waiting, assessing Ridley, biding his time, and that surprise attack was his strength, along with finely sharpened teeth and claws. So with the sun blazing high in the summer sky, Ridley had been sauntering through the long sweet grass without a care in the world until, out of nowhere, came the Fiend. It would have been a fight to the death - his death - if Percy hadn't come to his rescue. As it was the Fiend left him blind in one eye. But the loss of sight hadn't made him afraid to go hunting. The truth was he'd lost his nerve. Now he watched for every blade of twitching grass, cowered at every unexpected noise, and with every shuddering step he took he expected another fiendish ambush. He'd become a cowardly cat, afraid of his own shadow.

"You'll be all right, you know, Ridley. That horrible beast rarely comes hunting on your territory," said Percy.

"Only when I least expect him to," Ridley meowed.

"Henrietta the Hen will look after you."

"Thanks! Now I'm a cat who needs to be looked after by a chicken!"

Percy nuzzled the top of Ridley's head. "I know, you could come with me!" he said.

"If you think that's a good idea you've been eating too many fizzy apples, my horsey friend! Leave the safety of my rock and go on some crazy adventure! Have you gone mad?"

But all this talk of apples had made Ridley's tummy growl with hunger. He might as well get used to the feeling. Without Percy acting as lookout he'd never be safe going hunting again. How long did it take a cat to starve to death, he pondered, flicking a slug off his rock before it could slither over his paw? Perhaps he should have kept it. At least then he'd have something to eat. But by then the slug had vanished into the long grass. Ridley slumped down, ears drooping, and shut his eyes. "You go off and have a great time. Don't worry about me," he said.

"Don't be like that, Ridley. I have to go. It's the chance of a lifetime."

"So be it," said Ridley. "But let me tell you, my friend, some adventures can leave you scarred for life. Don't say I didn't warn you."

That evening Ridley watched the sun set, knowing that when it rose on a new day Percy would be racing off on some great adventure, without so much as a backward glance. While he, Ridley, would slowly starve to death on his rock, to be discovered years later, the desiccated corpse of a once fearless cat.

CHAPTER 2

A Change Of Plan

AS IT HAPPENED THERE WAS AN EARLY MORNING CHANGE of plan. Before the sun had even risen, Percy, too excited to sleep, went on a long gallop beneath the stars. But in front of the Ridley house he saw the flickering shadows of men, moving about. When he trotted closer to see what they were up to, he overheard Jasper Ridley and Harold talking about the day's plans.

Percy raced back to tell Ridley what he'd discovered, "Ridley! Wake up!" he shouted, unable to stop some dribble from splatting on Ridley's head.

"What? Is it raining? Oh, it's you."

"Yes, it's me. I have some very interesting news to tell you."

Ridley rolled over. "I'm surprised you're still here," he said, turning his back on Percy.

Ridley in a grump. Nothing new about that, so Percy ignored the snarl, and watched for the tell-tale twitch of Ridley's ears, which told him the cat was listening. Then he gave him the good news.

"I've just heard that Mr Obadiah Blackhart, Jasper's Butler, is travelling with us. He'll be going all the way to Southampton. But then, when we set off on our train journey to reach the great ship, Mr Blackhart will be coming home."

"How interesting. How I love to hear about Jasper's butler, a man who has called me, 'a worm-riddled flea-bag!' For all I care he can travel to the other side of the world and stay there!"

"Yes. Yes. It's very bad of him. Because you don't have fleas, not all year round anyway. And - well, er … I'm not sure about the worms. The thing is, Ridley, I'm not like you: I've never been on an adventure before, and between you and me, I'm feeling a bit nervous."

"I can tell."

"Really?"

"It's the way you keep spitting all over me."

"Right. Right. Must stop that. It would mean so much to me if a friend came with me for part of the journey, someone to wave me goodbye."

Ridley pretended to wash his fur. His heart picked up a pace, a little excited, but mainly afraid of what Percy might be asking him to do. "What's that got to do with me?" he said.

"You ... you're my friend. You are, aren't you, Ridley?"

Percy's ears had flattened against his head and his tail had gone all droopy. Ridley felt bad. He didn't mean to upset him. "Don't be daft!" he said. "I'm only teasing. Of course I'm your friend!"

"So you will come with me, just until Mr Blackhart turns back. There's a bit of a walk to Newcastle, then a steam train, which sounds exciting. When we catch our last train that takes us to the ship, you can travel back home with Mr Blackhart. He'll look after you, make sure that you're safe."

Ridley tried to imagine the butler looking after him. Many images came to mind, but not one that looked 'safe.' He paced up and down. A walk, a train, it all sounded unsettling, not at all like sitting safely at home on his rock. Unknown territory, that's what it was. Worse still, he imagined the moment he would have to say, 'goodbye' to Percy. He swallowed hard. But letting his one true friend set off on his great adventure without anyone to wave him goodbye seemed a terrible thing to do.

"All right," Ridley said, "For you - I'll do it."

But neither of them noticed the small cat hiding behind an ash tree, listening to every word. Archie-the-Fiend licked his lips and hissed with pleasure.

The first part of the farewell passed in a very jolly fashion, with Harold riding Percy, and Ridley marching along behind. The other men, all part of the Northumberland Hussars, seemed to like the idea of a cat travelling with them, and kept calling Ridley, 'our lucky cat,' which meant they fed him biscuits and cheese and tasty morsels all the way on the long train journey from Newcastle to Hampshire.

"You see, isn't this fun!" said Percy.

True enough, and Ridley had been having such a fun time that he felt strangely wrong-footed when the day came to say goodbye. But he thought of his rock, the green fields, all the familiar trees and lakes on the Blagdon Estate, the sight of the sun rising, the sun setting. Home called to him like an owl calling to its mate.

Ridley had no way of telling Mr Blackhart that he would be going home with him. Worse still, the butler kept rushing about like a man being chased by hornets. Ridley had trouble keeping track of him. When at last he caught sight of the man, he stuck to the butler's trouser leg as if he was woven from the same cloth.

"Stop rubbing your flea-ridden fur against my trouser leg!" Mr Blackhart said, giving Ridley a sharp kick with his pointed shoe.

After that all Ridley could do was trail after the butler like a mis-matched shadow. But the man could disappear as swiftly as a snake in the grass. Finally, though, the moment came when Ridley had to say 'goodbye' to Percy.

Led by Harold, Percy climbed on board the train that would take him to the big ship, and far away. His horsey friend looked so fine, a brave and happy stallion.

"Have a great adventure!" Ridley managed to squeak, before pretending to choke on a fur ball.

"Cough it up!" Percy laughed.

"Very funny!"

Percy snorted loudly, then stuck his head out of the train window. "Is that … is that Mr Blackhart?" he said.

"Where?"

"There! On that other train."

Ridley swung round just in time to catch Mr Obadiah Blackhart waving at him through the window.

"Quick Ridley! That's your train home," said Percy.

Ridley squeezed between a pair of boots, skidded across the platform, then ran as fast as his legs could carry him. But the butler's train was already moving, spurting its hot breath out of the top of its head. Its great wheels of iron turned faster. Ridley gasped, unable to keep up with it. All he could do was stand and watch as the train's last carriage sailed past him and vanished in a white cloud of steam.

Tongue lolling, Ridley panted hard. "I think I might be sick," he spluttered. He hadn't run that fast in a long time.

"Hello lucky cat," a soldier said, "Got a fur ball or something? Don't you worry, I'll help you onto the train. We wouldn't leave without you," and before Ridley had a chance to wriggle away, he'd been grabbed by the back of the neck and shoved through Percy's open window.

"You see, here's Percy's waiting for you. No need to panic old fellow.

"Old fellow! Old fellow! How dare you!" Ridley screeched. "I'm not old. I'm just a bit overweight!"

The train shunted forwards, let out a loud whistle. Steam swirled in through the open window making Ridley cough.

"Where? What? What's happening?" he spluttered.

Percy nuzzled his nose against the top of Ridley's head. "It looks as if you'll be coming on the great adventure with me after all!"

Ridley swallowed, choked on a mouthful of bile, and then fainted clean away.

CHAPTER 3

Lost At Sea

A BAD DREAM, THAT'S WHAT HE'D HAD: a most terrible dream, with the world rolling first one way then the other, sliding about as if the earth beneath him was no longer solid. Usually he loved sleeping in the stable curled up in Percy's warm blanket, but Ridley's head ached and he felt sick. Maybe he'd wrapped himself up too tightly. He crawled out from the blanket, stretched, and gave himself a shake. But he was still caught in his dream, with the stable moving, undulating, and he could hear a strange groaning. A weird sound, a bit like a horse trying to be sick.

Ridley blinked, pawed his bleary eyes. There was Percy, standing close by, a normal enough sight. Except something seemed very wrong with the picture in front of him this morning. Percy wasn't so much standing as swaying, and there seemed to be more than one Percy, several Percy-s, all different colours, all swaying. While, to the left of Percy's head, a blinding beam of daylight poured through a funny little round window that Ridley had never noticed before.

He let out a squeak. Then felt a bit ashamed of the noise, as it made him sound horribly like a mouse. Swallowing hard and trying not to be sick, in a more cat-like voice, he said, "What, in all of my nine lives is happening?"

Percy smiled a little, whinnied, then let out a long dangle of dribble, which swung from side to side.

"Oh! Oh dear!" Ridley said. This was no dream. Everywhere he looked there were horses, and the earth was moving, up and down, up and down. Ridley staggered over to where Percy was swaying, took one look at Percy's green and sweaty face, then threw up into his friend's water bucket.

"Ugh! Sorry!" Ridley moaned.

"It's a bit of a rough ride, isn't it," said Percy. "I'd like to do that, but horses can't be sick, so all I can do is sweat and dribble!"

"Lovely!" Ridley groaned.

"Maybe a sip of water will help you."

Ridley glanced at the contents of Percy's water bucket, and then threw up in it again.

"Better now? It's a bit of a wobbly start to our great adventure together, isn't it," Percy said.

Stabbing the wooden floor with his claws helped a bit, and rather than looking at all the other sweaty green-faced horses, it was better to keep his eyes on Percy's hoof. Stare at the three letters. HBR. Not look up. It stopped the world from swaying. He was trying to remember what had happened. Someone had shoved him through the train window, he remembered that much. After that he had no idea. He must have passed out or something. Well, no need to panic. Cats can always find their own way home.

"I'm sorry Percy, but I'm not coming on this adventure with you. As soon as this wretched train stops I'm going to leap off and go home to my rock," Ridley said, nearly falling over as the train lurched most peculiarly.

Percy gulped loudly, then coughed dribble all over the floor. "But we're not on a train, Ridley," he said. "This is the ship. We're sailing together, on the SS Minneapolis."

"This - isn't - a - train?"

"No, silly! Trains don't go up and down. You're lucky though. I had to be lifted onto the ship in some sort of a hoist. I was hanging in the air with my four legs dangling. Most undignified. But you were carried on board by Harold himself, carefully wrapped up tight in one of my blankets. Oh, you don't know how glad I am that you're coming with me!" Percy said.

As far as Ridley was concerned there was nothing to be glad about. He was a cat in a right pickle, and with only two choices left to him. He could stay clutching the floor beneath him and refuse to move until someone took him straight back home. Or, alternatively, he could take his chances, leap out of the round window and swim for it. He'd splashed across a deep puddle once and made it to the other side, but the sea looked to be an entirely different beast from a puddle. As he peered out of the round window he couldn't work out where the sea ended and the sky began. They kept swapping places. To land in the sea, did he need to leap up, or spring down? It was important to know, because he had a meagre enough chance of reaching home by swimming, and none whatsoever by attempting to fly. But before he could make his mind up, someone grabbed him by the scruff of the neck and lifted him into the air.

"I seem to be flying!" he screeched.

"Well, Harold, so this is the cat everyone's talking about," the man said. "Look, at his damaged left eye. Isn't he the cat that lives at Jasper's place? I'm sure I've seen him sitting on that big rock at the front of Jasper's house."

"Do you know, I think you're right," said Harold, grabbing hold of Ridley as if he was in a game of pass-the-parcel. "Jasper says their cat used to be an excellent rat-catcher, going off on adventures all over the estate. But now, for some unknown reason, the cat just sits on his rock most of the day, watching the world go by with his one good eye."

"Well in that case he's certainly a brave chap to come on this adventure with us."

"Isn't he just!" said Harold, handing Ridley back to the first man again. Back and forth, back and forth. Ridley would have hissed at them if he wasn't being half strangled.

"Do you know his name?"

"Afraid not. Why don't we name him after you?" said Harold.

"What, Major Philip?"

"No. I was thinking we could use the name all of your friends call you. Although, instead of just Peter, we could call the cat, Peter-the-Rock!"

"I like that! God named Peter the Apostle his rock, 'Thou art Peter, and upon this rock I will build my Church, and the gates of Hell shall not prevail against it.'" The Major held Ridley higher in the air.

"I'm not some hovering kestrel, you know!" meowed Ridley.

But the Major wasn't listening. He said, "I say unto you, brave cat, that whatever your name was before today, from now on you will be called Peter-the-Rock!"

"Even if a cat can't help the Northumberland Hussars to be stronger than their enemies, with a name like that he should bring our men luck. Let's hope so," said Harold, "because on this adventure we're going to need luck in abundance."

With the cheek of the devil the men then tickled Ridley under the chin. After being passed back and forth like a flagon of cider at a maypole dance, when they finally put him down, he found it hard to keep his balance. But thinking about his new name distracted him from being sick again, and as darkness crept in through the window, he was glad to curl up inside Percy's blanket and try to sleep. "I think I like my new name," he said.

"Peter-the-Rock. It's a very fine name. Strong and brave sounding, just like the cat you used to be," Percy said.

Yes, he had once been strong and brave, and his new name did make him feel a bit braver. But as for going with Percy, whether he had a new name or the old one, Ridley had given up adventures for good. The best place for him was home on his rock, and the sooner he was back there, the better. So when the evil ship stopped moving Peter-the-Rock, previously known as Ridley, planned to turn tail and run all the way home.

After all, Percy didn't need a cat to help him. He was a stallion, big and strong enough to look after himself.

CHAPTER 4

Nothing Like An Adventure

THE SHIP STOPPED. He'd made it as far as the gangplank when, in a swift piece of cat-kidnapping, the man named Harold snatched Peter up and bundled him into Percy's blanket.

"I want to go home!" Peter-the-Rock mewed.

But Harold plonked Peter onto a wooden cart. It jolted off at an alarming speed. The pile of wooden boxes beneath him kept shifting about, but with his four legs tangled up in the blanket Peter couldn't sink his claws in to keep a firm hold, so he kept bouncing up and down like a ball.

"Where are we going?" Peter shouted to Percy who was trotting along beside the cart.

"I don't know."

"How long will this adventure last?"

"I don't know. Relax. Enjoy yourself. Stop worrying!" Percy said.

"Are we there yet?" Peter snarled. What did Percy know about adventures? Nothing at all as it turned out. Because, after endless hours of being shaken up and down in a rickety wooden cart, Peter finally sprang free of his wrappings to find the destination of their grand adventure was a football pitch.

"This is it? We came all this way so you could nibble grass on a foreign football pitch?"

Percy stopped chewing, then shook his head, "This is Bruges."

"So are my buttocks from all that banging up and down in the cart!"

"No, silly, not bruise: Bruges."

"Well whatever this place is called, this is not an adventure. Someone's been lying to you."

"I know *this* isn't the adventure. I heard the Major telling Harold, 'this is where we wait'."

"Wait for what?"

"Wait for something to happen." Happy that he'd given Peter a good answer to his question, Percy went back to eating.

Standing watching Percy and all the other horses munching grass made Peter realise he hadn't had a decent meal in days. "Is that all there is to eat here? Grass?" he said.

"Goodness, I can hear your tummy roaring louder than those ocean waves! You could go and catch yourself a mouse now there's no Fiend to worry about. They might be tastier than the ones back home in Blagdon. Go on Peter-the-Rock, you brave, fearless cat you!" Percy snorted, then went back to munching his way across the football pitch.

At the sound of his new name Peter-the-Rock felt a sudden rush of courage. Percy was right. He'd left the Fiend far behind. The tall tufts of grass at the edge of the pitch looked a promising place for hunting. When a sudden movement caught his eye he set off at a run, glimpsed a sliver of tail, too long for a mouse though, too greyish, fattish, rattish. The rat caught the scent of cat, and swung round, baring its teeth. Yellow. Sharp. Definitely not a welcoming smile. Too sinister. Hungry-looking.

"You're back early!" Percy said. "Had yourself a tasty dinner?"

Peter shuddered. "Rats!" he said, "Giant rats." Even now they could be circling, closing in. From high up on his rock back home he'd had a view for miles around. Down on the ground he was as good as blind. Leaping back up onto the cart, tail flicking, he perched on top of the wooden boxes, an altogether safer position for sighting a rat about to lunge at his throat.

"I thought with your new name you were going to start being brave again."

"Shut up!" said Peter.

By sunset, Peter thought his stomach must have shrunk to nothing, but then Harold came to the rescue. The man turned out to be both kind and thoughtful, bringing Peter a big plateful of leftovers from the men's dinners.

"Want some?" Peter asked Percy.

"No thanks. This grass here is very tasty."

"Grass! Filthy stuff!" Peter said, gobbling up his dinner in case the rats got any thieving ideas.

The next day when they left Bruges, Peter happily waved the filthy rats 'goodbye.' But it was a long trudge to a place called Ostend. This town wasn't the destination of their adventure either, because the very next day off they went again. This time they were shoved onto some awful train, which chugged and spluttered, spewing filthy black smoke out of every orifice all the way to Ghent. But this seemed more like a place worth visiting. Here the men stayed in a lovely chateau, which meant 'a large country house', so it had lots of comfortable rooms. Peter wasted no time in curling up next to Harold on a comfy sofa, which turned out to be a very good idea as he was given more than one plate full of leftovers every evening.

Three days later, just when he'd made himself at home they set off on another very long walk, traipsing along dusty tracks, and over fields. Peter had noticed how the cart he travelled in seemed very important to Harold. Wherever Harold was, there was the cart. Peter liked this arrangement, because he was beginning to think of one or two questions to ask his horsey friend.

"Why are we moving again?"

"I'm not sure," said Percy.

"This is turning out to be a very peculiar sort of adventure, don't you think? Not that you know much about adventures. But every day nothing much happens, except I seem to be wearing down the pads of my paws by moving from one place to another."

"I see that."

"Why do we keep moving from place to place?"

"I don't know. I think it's to give us horses some exercise. We've gone a bit flabby after all that standing around on the ship."

But it seemed that the adventure had a few nasty surprises hidden up its sleeve.

It turned out that Harold and his friends were not on this adventure alone. There were Other Men.

Someone shouted, "They're coming!" and all hell broke out.

Harold leapt from Percy and started setting up a strange looking metal contraption that had been travelling alongside Peter's cart. Four other men raced to help him. A machine gun, the men called it. Peter didn't like the smell of it one bit. And nor did Percy. One man shoved Peter to one side and opened some of the wooden boxes that he'd been sitting on and pulled out a long lumpy belt. Once they'd attached the belt to the gun, Harold yelled, "Ready!" and then there was the most terrifying RAT-TAT-TAT-TAT-TAT! Percy leapt high into the air.

"Private Bainbridge! Look after my horse," shouted Harold.

A kind-looking man, short and neat, came running forwards and grabbed hold of Percy's reins. He tried his best to keep him steady, while Harold ran off, moving the gun from the first place, setting it up again, firing it - RAT-TAT-TAT-TAT-TAT! - then moving it again. The noise frightened Percy half to death. No amount of patting his neck, or saying "Sorry!" in his ear could calm him. A glimpse of the Other Men, a blue shirt, a glint of metal, and RAT-TAT-TAT-TAT-TAT! off the gun went again.

If that wasn't terrible enough, the Other Men started making a noise as well. *KERBOOMF! KERBOOMF!* Bits of trees shattered. The very earth leapt up into the air to shower down on them like rain. Peter slunk under the cart, too terrified to help Percy. He shut his eyes, tried to imagine home with the sound of the breeze and the birds and perfect peace. But, BOOM! RAT-TAT-TAT-TAT-TAT! *KERBOOMF!* on it went, the same thing, all the long day. Harold would ride Percy a short distance, leap off, fire his gun, BOOM! RAT-TAT-TAT-TAT-TAT! *KERBOOMF!* Ride some more, fire his gun, on and on and on. Peter had no idea what Harold was trying to do. None of this made any sense. And these Other Men, who were they? What did they want?

Exhausted, they staggered on until finally they reached a pretty place called Ypres. Harold slumped down onto Percy's back. He didn't even have the strength to dismount, so Private Bainbridge lent a hand, half carrying Harold to his make-shift bed in one of a row of tents that had been hastily erected by the weary men. As for Percy, he stood on trembling legs with his head hanging down.

Peter nuzzled his friend with his nose. "Are you all right, Percy?" he said.

"This is a strange adventure, isn't it?" said Percy.

"Yes. Yes it is," said Peter.

"I … I … perhaps I'll feel better after a good sleep."

But it seemed that the Other Men never slept, which meant that everything went from bad to worse.

CHAPTER 5

From Bad To Worse And Back Again

FILTHY AND TIRED, like rats in a rat run, the men scuttled along the trenches. Weary enough already, it didn't matter who they were, officer, foot soldier, all of the men had had to lend a hand digging these shallow channels in the earth. When the trenches were finished the men without horses were told to jump in, but their heads stuck out over the top, leaving their ears vulnerable to the icy cold wind and all of them at the mercy of the KERBOOMFS that set earth and trees flying at their heads. The walls of the trenches couldn't be trusted either. The sides kept collapsing in without warning, showering the men in a storm of sticky mud. The real rats, of course, felt quite at home. They ran up and down the trenches all day, stealing whatever food they could find, gnawing on the men's shoes and clothing with their sharp teeth.

Peter shook himself, trying to fling off the mud that stuck to his fur. He longed to run across a field, climb a tree, feel the warm sun on his shivering skin. But danger lurked everywhere. He had never known such a terrible place, or such long days, burdened with the same monotonous routine. A shout would go up. As soon as they heard it, the men staggered up out of the trenches, marching forwards in rigid lines towards where the Other Men were hiding. The two sides seemed to be playing a funny sort of game of hide-and-seek. Men fell over from time to time. Some of them didn't bother to stand up again, which meant that the neat little line suddenly had a gap in it. It seemed to be Harold's job, together with the other men on horses, to race over as quickly as they could to fill the gap. But the dense trees that made up the Polygon Wood made it hard for anyone to see where the Other Men were, or what they were up to. A strange business indeed.

And all the while the screaming BOOM! RAT-TAT-TAT-TAT-TAT! *KERBOOMF!* rang in everyone's ears. Every so often Peter dared to take a peek, but quickly returned to the safest position he could find, hiding under his cart. He tried covering his eyes so that he couldn't see anything. Then he covered his ears, so that he couldn't hear anything. Ears, eyes. Ears, eyes. But even with his ears flattened and muffled by his paws, the sound of Percy's whinnying reached him, and no matter how tightly he screwed up his eyes, the sight of Percy's face remained vivid in his mind. Percy, the brave stallion, his nostrils flaring, eyes white with terror.

Peter peeked out again. Percy stood not far off, right in the thick of it. Then Harold rose up in his stirrups, pointed deeper into the wood, and off they charged again. Private Bainbridge grabbed Peter's cart and started dragging it, racing after Harold.

"Howay, canny cat! Jump on board!"

Peter didn't want to lose sight of his friend, and the cart always followed Harold, so he leapt on top and hunkered low. Horses were charging this way and that, swerving, then charging the other way. He wondered if anyone knew what was happening. Willing himself not to flinch at every loud noise, Peter kept sight of Percy, up ahead, not far away now. But then a dreadful thing happened right in front of Peter's eyes. He'd heard a whizz, followed by a pop. The man on the nearest horse must have heard them too, because he slumped forwards as if he could somehow duck underneath the sounds. For a moment he lay along his horse's back, resting his head between the animal's ears like he needed a bit of a sleep. But then he slid off sideways, hit the ground and lay there, not moving. A red liquid spread around his chest, staining his jacket. But he didn't try to wipe it off. He didn't move at all. His horse didn't move either. The poor creature just stood there, staring into the distance. Maybe it couldn't run off because the man still had hold of the horse's reins in his left hand.

Private Bainbridge glanced at the man, but didn't stop to help him up. With one fierce tug he set his cart moving faster, nearly toppling Peter off, and caught up with Harold and Percy.

As he cowered beneath the cart, Peter thought about that red stain, what it might mean. He thought about it long and hard. When, at last, he understood, his tail flopped down and his ears lay flat against his head.

"This isn't an adventure," he whispered, and the beat of his heart pounded all the way to the end of his nose.

Surely he must be wrong? The conclusion he'd come to seemed too terrible to be true, much better to believe that the two groups of men were playing a game of hide-and-seek. But when more men fell to the ground and didn't get up, Peter let out a low growl.

"They are killing each other," he said. "Why would they want to do such a terrible thing?"

Crawling out from his hiding place beneath the cart, trembling and bewildered Peter stared at the terrible world he saw in front of him.

"This is no place for a cat," he said.

Beyond the trees and the men and the horses there must be another world. Once he reached it, he could run and run and never stop until he was home again. No one would pay any attention to him. Besides, a cat has nine lives.

So he set off, weaving his way through the men, half running, half stumbling, tripping over broken branches, swerving around the horses and the men mired in the mud. He reached a dense hedge, a prickly blackthorn, tugged his way through it, feeling the thorns tearing flesh. But he didn't care. He could sense the fresher air tingling on the tip of his tongue, and in the distance he could hear a lonely blackbird calling. Fields, he saw them, beckoning to him, luscious green and full of hope. Peter broke free of the thorns and raced towards them.

But as he ran a truly terrible thought came into his head. The Other Men wanted to kill Harold. If they wanted to kill Harold, they would think nothing of killing Percy. Peter stopped. His tongue felt as if someone had smothered it in dry dust. Percy, dead. He could never let that happen. Harold kept firing his gun like a blind man, with no idea of where the Other Men were hiding. But what if Peter helped Harold play his deadly game, and helped him to win?

Suddenly his legs felt as wobbly as a newborn lamb's, but they were the only legs he had, so Peter pounded the earth with them, racing back to the Polygon Wood.

He spotted Private Bainbridge and his cart first, and then he saw Percy. Relief spread through him like warming rays of sunshine. Harold was busy setting up his gun again, but through the tangle of trees there was no way he could see the Other Men. But still he aimed his gun, hoping for the best.

In times of trouble a cat takes to the high ground. Peter saw the perfect pine tree. Huffing and puffing, he made his way to the very top, then sat there for a moment, needing to catch his breath.

"I'm not as fit as I used to be!" he mumbled.

From on high he could see for miles. The Polygon Wood must have been a wonderful place once, before the men had arrived to play their strange games. But now the limbs of many trees lay shattered, their ancient trunks blasted to pieces, so that the oaks and aspens still standing in their glorious autumn colours of glimmering gold, looked out of place in all of the carnage. Far in the distance he could see the blackthorn hedge and the fields of green, the long grasses waving to him, full of the promise of home. But he mustn't think about home now. Peter could see Harold dragging the machine gun into position, all the while peering through the trees, trying to see what he couldn't see. But Peter could see the Other Men clearly, and he could see that Harold was aiming his gun too far to the left.

Peter sprang out, claws extended, and leapt to the next tree. Scratching and sliding to gain a good grip of a branch, he then scrambled down the trunk. Peter ran over to the gun and scuffed a line in the earth with his paws. The line led from the gun's mouth, pointing not to the left, but at a sharp angle to the right, aiming directly at where the Other Men were hiding. Harold was too busy to notice, but meowing like the worst spoilt cat made Private Bainbridge turn and look.

"Sir!" Private Bainbridge said. "Tha moggie, Peter-the-Rock, he's trying te git ya attention wi aal tha meowing. Ah think he's trying te tell yee summat. That's a cle-ah line he's making in the dirt, leik he wants yee te aim yer gun more te the reet."

"He's just a cat," Harold muttered.

"Aye. But I've seen him, climbing tha' tree. Maybe he saw summat wi canna see."

"Oh why not!" said Harold. "I can't see a damn thing! Help me adjust the gun!

Hurry now!"

So they aimed the gun more to the right and fired, just in time to hit a cluster of the Other Men as they appeared through the trees with their rifles aimed at Harold and his men.

"Well, Peter-the-Rock! You are our lucky cat and no mistake!" said Harold.

CHAPTER 6

No Going Back

PETER HAD NO IDEA HOW LONG the two sides meant to keep up all of the killing. A cat kills a mouse to eat it. This seemed to be about something else entirely. Just a single day of all the continuous BOOM! RAT-TAT-TAT-TAT-TAT! *KERBOOMF!* had made him feel sick to his guts. But on it went, day after day, and often through the long nights too. While the men grew thinner the scavenging rats grew fatter, the only creatures thriving in these strange times.

On some nights, though, the guns fell silent and the men left all the killing to the hungry owls and the foxes. On these nights, too exhausted to speak, in silence the men crawled out of their trenches, ate what little they had, and tried to catch some sleep in the relative comfort of their tents. Hard though. By now the men were riddled with lice, so their skin itched all the long night as they huddled together for warmth wrapped in their filthy blankets.

But on these quiet nights, when Harold thought it would be safe, he would come over to where all the horses were tied to the rope, thread through a series of picket spikes. Setting Percy free, he checked him over for muddy patches and sores. When he was certain that he'd been thoroughly groomed and was as healthy as he could be, he would sit with Percy and Peter, and in the dim light of the oil lamp he'd set about writing a letter to his wife. Peter enjoyed those nights because Harold would always read his letters out loud as he wrote them, as if checking to see if horse and cat approved.

Harold had brought with him one photograph of his family. Safely tucked between the pages of his prayer book, which he kept in the inside pocket of his jacket, the photograph nestled close to his heart. But when Harold wrote his letters home he would pull out the photograph, study the faces of his wife and little son, William, and placing the photograph by his side he would begin to write. Peter liked the look of Harold's wife. She had a kind face, and his son had a lovely big smile.

One star filled night Harold wrote this letter:

'My dear Ysolt, What an exciting experience we all had today, though not entirely free from an uncomfortable feeling, what with bullets and shells whizzing past.'

Harold stopped writing and looked up, "Best I don't tell her the truth. I have to make light of it all. You both agree with that, don't you?" Harold said, giving Peter a little scratch between the ears. "But this next bit is true: *'I know you worry about me, my darling, but there's no need, because Percy keeps me safe and out of trouble. He's fast and brave and does everything I ask of him. And Peter-the-Rock has become our clever scout, finding the enemy for us every day. He's not just a lucky cat, but a fearless one too. So you see, I am in safe hands.'"*

Harold looked up, shook his head. "This is a terrible war, boys," he said, slipping the photograph back between the pages of his prayer book, "and I'm just an ordinary man, no different from all of the other men who've come here to fight against the Germans. Some days all of this bloodshed makes me feel sick to my stomach. But then I remember why I'm fighting." With his prayer book now safely tucked deep in his pocket, he rested his hand on his heart. "I'm fighting to keep the people I love safe. And because I'm protecting the ones I love it gives me the courage I never knew that I had."

Long after Harold had returned to his tent to sleep, Peter lay on his back watching for shooting stars and thinking of home.

"There's the North Star!" he said. "Do you see it, Percy, that small star balanced on the tail of the Little Bear?"

But Percy didn't answer. He was trying to doze. But it was hard for either of them to sleep, because a noisy scops owl kept flying about, swooping near, then flying off again. Back and forth it flew, all the while calling. It sounded as if the owl kept saying, "Twerp! Twerp!" A scops owl endlessly calling a person, 'silly or stupid,' made perfect sense to Peter as he lay there, thinking about the crazy war and the pickle they were all in.

"That's a very silly and stupid owl, don't you think?" Percy said.

"My thoughts, exactly," Peter yawned.

"Harold is wrong about me, you know. I'm not brave at all," said Percy.

"And I'm not fearless," said Peter.

"But it's nice that Harold believes we're brave and fearless, and that he thinks we're really helping him."

"Yes," said Peter.

"I really want to help Harold."

"Me too," said Peter.

"I wouldn't want anything - you know - anything bad to happen to Harold. He's such a kind man, trying to keep the people he loves safe. That's such a brave thing to do."

Peter nodded. What if Archie-the-Fiend, or some other monster, tried to attack Percy? Could he be as brave as Harold? He doubted it.

After a long silence Percy sighed. "Peter, I'm so sorry," he said.

Peter stretched a little, gave another yawn, wished he could fly, catch the noisy little scops owl and eat it. It was the only way he could think of to shut it up. "Sorry for what?" he said.

"This isn't a great adventure. This is a terrible place I've brought you to, and … and I'm very afraid we'll never see our home again."

Peter swallowed hard. With his eyes closed he could still imagine skylarks flying high, singing at the top of their voices. Across the green fields that stretched all the way from the Ridley House to the horizon, cows and sheep would be moving gently, mooing and baaing happily. But best of all, with his eyes tightly shut, he could almost feel the sun on his face and imagine long, summer days, stretched out on his rock, and Percy galloping across the meadow in a world of perfect peace. To never see his home again: he couldn't bear to think of such a thing.

"It's all right, Percy. Don't you worry," Peter said, trying not to let the tremor of doubt creep into his voice. "We'll be all right. We've got Harold. He'll make sure that we all return home safely. You know he will."

But the scops owl cried, "Twerp! Twerp! Twerp!"

CHAPTER 7

Rat Hunting

WINTER TOOK A VICIOUS HOLD OF THE LAND, giving men, horses and cat more enemies to fight than just the Germans. Mud, black and sticky and cold as death, clung to everything. The never-ending rain filled the trenches with icy water, which seeped through boots and clothes and fur, freezing everyone to the bone. The trenches that offered little enough cover from flying bullets, gave no shelter at all from the cruel weather. The men grew thin, and cold, and sick. Food that was already rationed needed to be rationed some more.

But then Christmas Day came, bringing with it a magical power beyond Peter's imagining. When Harold and his men laid down their weapons and tethered their horses, so did the Other Men. Every gun fell silent, and one by one the men climbed out of their trenches. Instead of killing each other, they came together on the muddy field. Private Bainbridge had a ball, so the men played football together, laughed and shoved each other, scored goals against each other and cheered the winning side. Then a German soldier started singing *Silent Night*. It didn't seem to matter that he sang in a foreign language, Harold and his men joined in anyway. After that they all shook hands, exchanged gifts - a cigarette, a piece of chocolate - as if the game of war had never been played.

Watching them gave Peter a pain in his heart. Percy whinnied as if he felt the same. Christmas would soon be over, and then the men must return to their trenches, and the terrible war would begin all over again. Percy would need all of his strength to help Harold, but he'd grown so thin. His ribs stuck out, so that he looked more like a carcass hanging in a butcher's window than a horse.

"Happy Christmas!" Percy said.

"Yes, happy Christmas," said Peter. "I don't seem to have a gift to give you! Sorry about that!"

"Ha!" Percy snorted. "Harold's wife sent him some lovely socks for Christmas though, don't you think?"

"No. You can't eat socks!" Peter growled.

Percy didn't answer. The once powerful stallion didn't bother to talk much these days. Although Harold and Private Bainbridge had tried their best to keep Percy in good health, no one could fail to notice that his once shiny chestnut coat looked dull and patchy, even when it wasn't matted with grey clumps of mud. There was no grass left. Private Bainbridge told Peter that the Germans had run out of hay and were feeding their horses on sawdust. Percy was fed some hay to keep him going, but as a horse needs to eat ten times as much food as a man, a bit of hay now and then would never be enough.

"I'm sorry, Percy," Peter said, "I didn't mean to snap. I know you're just as hungry as me."

"Everyone's hungry but the rats," said Percy, then he hung his head pretending to be dozing. But in truth he was often too weary to sleep.

"Is there anything I can do to help you, my friend?" Peter said.

"My dear Peter, I haven't the slightest idea." Percy said without bothering to open his eyes. He had the look of a horse who'd given up.

The rats - Percy was right - they weren't hungry, not in the least. Every day they scuttled along the trenches, then up and out, racing across the fields, gobbling up anything they could sink their yellow teeth into. The thought of all those rats feasting while Percy starved made Peter's tail twitch. Well if the rats could hunt and eat, so could he. He set off for a scout around, looking for any scraps. There were bits and pieces, rotten and wriggling with maggots. But nothing a horse might like to eat.

But Peter didn't give up. And then, he got lucky. At first he thought there must be something wrong with his eyes. He blinked, looked again, and it was still there: a whole apple, rosy, red. The only problem was, a rat had found the apple first. And not just any rat: a rat the size of a cat.

Peter froze. The stink of rat awakened a dim rat-hunting memory; that it was best to act quickly before the rat caught wind of him. Or worse still before it slunk down its rat hole and disappeared with the juicy apple. With the fruit firmly gripped in its yellowing teeth, the rat could run fast. But Peter followed behind like a faithful shadow. It must have lost its sense of smell, because it didn't notice him. Not at first, anyway. But half way across the muddy field the rat stopped, dropped the apple, and sniffed the air. Now or never, Peter thought. Claws out, he pounced, one paw swiping the rat sideways as he grabbed the apple in his teeth. But, quick as a flea, the rat jumped up, teeth bared, and leapt onto Peter's back. He remembered this was their favourite trick, so before it could sink its fangs into his neck, he threw himself onto his back, crushing the wind out of the rat. Then he snatched up the apple and ran.

Rats never give up either. When he felt its hot breath burning the back of his legs he realised the time had come to remember who he'd once been. Long ago, before he'd become a coward, he'd made his reputation on Ridley lands as the only cat brave enough to fight huge rats. Dropping the apple onto a cluster of dandelion leaves, he swung round.

"My friend needs this apple, and I'm going to make sure he gets it!" he snarled. With teeth and claws at the ready, Peter-the-Rock did what he had to do.

Not wishing to startle the sleeping horse, Peter whispered, "Percy! Percy!"

"Huh? Peter. Goodness, you smell really awful!"

"Yes. Sorry. I had a bit of a run-in with a rat. I don't think rats like all these sudden noises! RATA-BOOM-POP-WHIZ! He seemed a little bit crazy!"

"Is that a scratch on your cheek?"

"Never mind that. Look, Percy! I've brought you an apple. A whole apple. It's a bit bruised but it's still tasty."

"Mmmm. It smells so much better than you!"

"Munch it all down. Take your time. Eat slowly. You haven't eaten anything for days, and you don't want to make yourself sick."

"Come on, Peter, we'll share it."

"No, Percy. It's all for you. You don't need to worry about me. I've already eaten."

CHAPTER 8

A Change For The Better

"LOOKS LEIK WE'RE GUNNA HEV A CHANGE of scenery, lads!" Private Bainbridge said.

Peter meowed, wanting to know more, and Private Bainbridge obliged.

"I'd betta smarten yee both up canny good an proper. We're aal gunna Italy, which I hear is a pretty fancy place."

After more than three years of Ypres, Peter and Percy held their breath, wondering what this Italy might look like, whether it would mean just more mud and lice and rats.

When they reached their destination Peter ran round and round in circles, hairs bristling with excitement. "Is this Italy?" he shouted, finding it difficult to believe his eyes.

"Steady Peter! You don't want to shake off all that luck you're bringing us!" said Harold, grinning from ear to ear, and slapping Private Bainbridge on the back.

Harold, Private Bainbridge, the horse and the cat all breathed a sigh of relief. The mud and squalor of Ypres had clung to them day and night, weighing them down. But here, fields of luscious green grass covered the land, and majestic mountains rose up so high that Peter thought their tops must touch the sky. The wide and bountiful river, named the Piave, seemed to sing to them as it meandered past on its way to the sea.

"Smile!" Harold said, pulling out his camera to take their photograph.

"Look!" he pointed across the river. "There! You can see the medieval tower of Padua shining like gold, and that one must be Verona. Isn't this place marvellous!"

Peter watched Harold strolling about, taking photographs of every corner of this new world as if they were having a picnic on a Sunday afternoon.

"This is not just a change of scenery. This is heaven!" Peter said to a blue butterfly that happened to flutter by. He breathed in the scent of spring and the taste of home.

The fighting went on all right, but the men weren't stuck in those terrible trenches, so for everyone the world became a more bearable place. Harold smiled more, and looked less gaunt and grey. Nibbling away to his heart's content on all the spring grass, Percy fattened up, so his coat took on a healthy shine for the first time in three years. Fish swam in the river, and scrawny chickens ran about. The soldiers ate well, eggs and cheese and milk, not a feast, but enough, and Harold and Private Bainbridge always made sure they ate most of the food on their plate, but left a little bit for Peter. But Peter was already well fed. He spent the sunny days chasing mice through the long grass, or doing a bit of light fishing, before retiring for an afternoon of sunbathing. And with each passing day the hope grew stronger in his heart that they might survive after all. One day soon they would all go home.

But six months later horses, men and a cat all crowded onto a railway platform. They were on the move again. Italy had been a brief holiday, that was all. Suspicious of trains, Peter took to the high ground. Sitting on Percy's back, he watched Harold talking to a man he'd never seen before.

"What do you mean?" Harold spoke with a calm voice, but his face looked worried.

The man shook his head. "Sorry, Sir," he said, "but you can see for yourself - the trains are stuffed full of men. It's not just your horse. There isn't room for any of the horses."

"How will I be able to fight the Germans without my horse?" Harold said. The man shrugged.

After that Peter found it hard to think straight. Harold abandoning Percy? He would never do such a thing. But Harold beckoned to Private Bainbridge, and after that everything happened so quickly.

"It's all right," Harold said, stroking Percy and talking low in his ear. Then he stroked Percy one last time, stepped back and handed Private Bainbridge the reins.

With his arms held rigid by his sides and the frown on his face deepening, Harold said, "Bainbridge, I know you're a good man. I trust you to do your very best. Look after Percy. Keep him safe. Do you hear me?"

"Aye, sir. Ye can rely on me, sir. Divvent yee worry yourself. Ah can dee that. Nay trouble."

"I think it's best if Peter stays with you. Our lucky cat can help you the way he's been helping me. I think that's what Peter-the-Rock would want to do," Harold said, stroking Peter between the ears. "Well, I'd best be off. I don't like this, I don't like this one little bit. I thought we'd made enough of a mess of Ypres last time, but I'm sorry to say it looks like we're going to get the chance to destroy the place completely. The western front won't seem the same without my friends to help me."

Peter, Percy and Private Bainbridge stood staring after Harold as he boarded the train. Then, with a cough of smoke, the train disappeared under a grey cloud and was gone, taking Harold with it, back to the awful place that Peter hoped none of them would ever see again.

Percy whinnied, lost his footing.

"Are you all right, Percy?" Peter said.

"Harold will never manage without me," Percy whinnied again.

"Don't worry, Percy. Harold is brave. He'll be fine."

"No he won't. Not without me to help him, and you to scout for him."

"It's no good whinnying. No matter how much noise you make, they won't let us on the train," said Peter.

"Then we'll have to get on the train without them seeing us!"

"May I remind you that you are a horse, not a flea!" said Peter.

"And may I remind you that you are a very clever cat, so think of something!"

In the end Private Bainbridge, a canny Geordie man, was way ahead of them.

"Reet yee two. Wi aal knaa we need te get on tha train. So listen carefully. This is what wi need te dee."

CHAPTER 9

A Great Adventure Indeed

THE PLAN WENT WELL. At least to start with. Private Bainbridge never doubted for a moment that both the cat and the horse understood every word that he said to them. Peter thought that was very unusual for a man. But as time went by he discovered that Private Bainbridge believed many things were possible that others thought impossible. This was a man who never doubted, or gave up. In fact, Peter concluded that Private Bainbridge would have made a very fine cat, which would have been better than being a man as he would have been blessed with a cat's lucky nine lives.

The plan was clear. It went like this: men were still boarding the last train, so Peter's job was to cause chaos on the station platform. That way all eyes would focus on him, instead of on a chestnut horse sneaking onto the last carriage of the train. Peter managed to find a very large rat lurking in the shadows. It wasn't difficult to find, because fat rats lurked everywhere. Rats don't like to have their tails pulled, or their bottoms nipped or be pawed by a cat. So Peter pulled the rat's tail, then nipped its bottom and batted it about a bit with his paws. The other rats didn't like Peter messing with their friend, so several came out of their rat hole to join in the game. In no time at all a neat line of rats were chasing Peter along the station platform. But he didn't mind. A slimmer cat now, he felt more like his old Lion-self again, light on his paws, moving swiftly. Every so often he let out a roar! at a rat that came too close. He realised he hadn't had this much fun in ages.

Peter knew that men liked rats even less than cats like rats. So just as he'd hoped, the men started yelling and jumping, leaping out of the way and flinging their luggage at the rats. Sometimes they missed a rat and nearly hit a cat. But apart from that, all in all Private Bainbridge's plan worked perfectly. While all eyes glared at Peter and the rats,

Private Bainbridge and Percy climbed unobserved into the last carriage, squeezing in between the machine guns and the ammunitions boxes. The train hooted, a cloud of smoke billowed, at which point Peter realised that the wretched train was setting off without him. Running and leaping, he managed to catch up with the last carriage just as two of the meanest-looking rats caught up with him. The sight of their bared teeth gave him the extra burst of speed he needed just as Private Bainbridge, lying on his belly, reached out to grab Peter by the scruff of the neck.

"Gotcha, you brave and clever moggie!" he said, hauling Peter aboard.

They congratulated each other, laughed and congratulated each other a bit more, and then settled down for a long journey.

A little while later they discovered the unexpected flaw in the plan. The train had reached its destination, and everyone clambered off. But the destination turned out to be nowhere near Ypres.

Private Bainbridge scratched his head. "Hmm," he said "Ah canna lie te ye. Ah expected the train te gan a bit furtha than this. But Lyon is weor we are, like. So aal we need te dee is figure oot hoo te get from here te Ypres."

With that he pulled a small brass object from his jacket pocket. "Teka lyeuk at this compass, lads," he said, beckoning them closer.

Peter and Percy peered at the small instrument nestling in the palm of Private Bainbridge's hand. It looked like a watch, but instead of two hands it had an arrow that kept spinning one way, and then the other.

"Ah knaa Ypres is North. See how this arrow is pointing North? So aal wi hev te dee is follow the arrow an' we'll be walking North. Easy as drinkin a pint of beeah!"

Later Peter wondered if, at the moment when they all gazed at the spinning arrow, Private Bainbridge had any idea of how many miles they would need to walk before they reached Ypres. But perhaps it was better that none of them knew when they set out from Lyon that there were four hundred and fifty long, weary miles ahead of them.

"Are we there yet?" Peter said every time they turned a bend in the path and saw more empty space stretching out in front of them. Yet each day they began to feel better, stronger. They ate well, drank fresh water from fast flowing streams, felt the warm sun on their faces, and tasted clean air with each breath. But that didn't stop them from worrying about Harold. How was he doing without them? How many more miles would they need to walk before they reached him?

"A bit of youthful poaching taught me a lot of hunting skills, leik," said Private Bainbridge one evening as they gathered round a small fire. He prodded the rabbit that Peter had caught earlier that day to see if it was cooked. "Mainly I learnt that a bit of poaching is a canny good deal betta than starving." The rabbit was small, but it would be enough of a meal. Even when they caught sight of a deer sniffing the air or grazing close by, Private Bainbridge didn't shoot it. Gunfire might attract too much attention from the wrong people. But he knew how to light a good fire and cook a tasty meal with whatever he could find, and Peter relished the opportunity to help out, each success reawakening in him his own hunting skills. While Peter and Private Bainbridge shared a dinner, Percy enjoyed his favourite meal of grass.

They knew they had to be careful though. The sound of booming guns could always be heard, so if they glimpsed a stranger Private Bainbridge would lead Percy into the shadows to hide.

"Ah divvent speak French. You'll hev te dee the taakin, Peter," he'd say.

Peter knew what that meant. So he'd turn on his moggy charm, circling the stranger's legs, purring like a lonely, affectionate cat, but all the while trying to figure out if this person might be friend or foe. When he couldn't be sure, he would walk a while with them, doing his best to be amusing, until he knew Private Bainbridge and Percy had moved a safe distance away, further along the path. Then, when the stranger wasn't looking, he'd slip away and run off to catch up with his friends. One time he met an old man who was so glad of the company, he gave Peter a tasty piece of fish to eat. Peter started to drool, it smelt so good. For a moment he thought of gobbling it all down. No one would know. But that would make him a greedy cat. Even when they'd been starving, the men had shared their food with him. So, trying not to dribble on it, he carried the piece of fish back to share it with Private Bainbridge for dinner.

When the path was narrow or treacherous with shifting rocks and slippery scree, Private Bainbridge led the way and horse and cat walked behind him. Most of the time, though, Private Bainbridge and Peter rode on Percy's back because that way they could travel more quickly. But no matter how heavy his burden, Percy never complained.

"Soon we'll see Harold," he kept saying.

Perhaps ten days had gone by, perhaps more. They'd lost count. With the mountains far behind them now, they'd spent the night sleeping huddled together, hidden in a small copse by a stream. But at the darkest part of the night, just before the dawn, the bitter cold had woken them. After eating some breakfast they'd waited a while, setting off as soon as there was enough light to see where they were going. They hadn't travelled far before they turned a sharp bend in the path and, in his usual way, Peter said, "Are we there yet?"

He waited for Percy to say, "not yet."

Instead his friend whinnied gently, snorted with excitement and said, "Yes! Look!"

Every day they had imagined this moment, but after walking four hundred and fifty miles the sight was so unexpected. But they had finally arrived. In the strange, dawn light that makes the world seem hazy and unreal, Peter saw the familiar line of tents, and beyond them the trenches. As if he couldn't work out how to take the next step, Private Bainbridge's feet stopped moving. Together they stood in silence, watching the sun rise. Slowly it spread its blood-red light over a scene of devastation. Private Bainbridge shook his head, turned away as if to catch his breath. Four years ago, when they had first arrived at Ypres, it had been a prosperous and elegant town surrounded by green fields and woodlands. Now, there was nothing left to see except shards of shattered trees lying beside the bodies of men, half buried in the muddy ruins of a place utterly destroyed by war.

Percy whinnied. "Look!" he said. "There's Harold!"

CHAPTER 10

Nearly The End Of Everything

HAROLD COULDN'T BELIEVE HIS EYES when he saw them. It took him days before he stopped shaking Private Bainbridge's hand and saying, "I don't know how you sneaked a horse onto a train!" and then, "I don't know how you walked all the way from Lyon to Ypres!" and, "I can't tell you how very glad I am to see you!"

Harold told them all his news too, that the Other Men were steadily being driven back and that, at this rate, the fighting might come to an end soon. Plus Harold had been promoted. He was now an aide-de-camp, which sounded very fancy, although Peter had no idea what it meant. Luckily it made no difference to their lives. Harold still looked after them, and they still looked after Harold. Except now Private Bainbridge became an indispensible member of their team.

Then the great day finally arrived. The war was over. The Other Men had lost. They were defeated, beaten, and sent packing.

"Well lads, it looks leik we'll aal be gannin hyem soon!" said Private Bainbridge.

Home. Peter's ears twitched with excitement. "Percy, just imagine, home. There'll be so much grass for you to eat you'll be as fat as one of those rats!"

Percy smiled, but not a big enough smile. Something was up, Peter could tell. "Aren't you excited?" he said.

"I don't want to think too much about home until we're truly there. And anyway …"

"Anyway, what?"

"It's Harold," said Percy.

"What about him?"

"He doesn't look right. I'm worried about him."

"He looks fine to me. Happy as a skylark!" said Peter.

But that evening, when Harold sat with them to write his letter home, Peter nuzzled up against him and took a good look at his face. Maybe it was the lamplight casting shadows over his skin that made Harold's lips look blue and his cheeks all speckled with dark spots.

"Hello Peter-the-Rock, our lucky cat. Are you keen to know what I'm telling my wife about you? Well, I'm telling her how we couldn't have won this war without you. You and Percy, a cat and a horse, have helped us to keep our loved ones safe from harm. You know that don't you. And look what I've written here, *soon, my darling, we will all be coming home.'*"

The next morning Private Bainbridge brought them the news. In the night Harold had complained of a headache and a slight fever, and had taken to his bed. But soon it became clear that Harold was gravely ill. He had the Spanish flu. They were sending him home, leaving Percy and Peter at Ypres without him.

"But dona worry, yee two. I'll look affta yee. An yee, Percy, you're a lucky horse leik! You're gannin on a victory parade, riding fine as the day through Brussels. Harold canna be there, but a canny good gadgie, Lieutenant Richard Tolson will be riding yee."

The Victory Parade was glorious. Peter felt sad that Harold had missed it, all the music and laughter, and the sight of men smiling and cheering and the crowds cheering back, waving flags, everyone happy. Peter climbed a flagpole, meowing and waving his tail as Percy rode by. Percy looked so fine, and soon they would be home, and Percy could gallop across the fields while Peter sun-bathed on his rock.

But after they returned from the Victory Parade Private Bainbridge was waiting for them.

"I've come to say, goodbye," he said.

He'd been given orders. He was on the next train out.

"Ah divvunt want te leave yee leik this, an nor did Harold. But orders is orders. Yees two stick together, and soon ye'll be back hyem at Blagdon and I'll be straight o'er to see yee. You'll be sunbathing on tha rock of yours, Peter, an you'll be rolling in the long grass, Percy. Just stick together, ye hear me, and you'll be hyem soon."

CHAPTER 11

One Last Ride

THERE WERE SO MANY MEN, pushing and shoving, all trying to squeeze into every available space on the four trains. The horses had been tied to a fence, waiting in a line with their heads facing away from the station platform. Percy was the last to be tied up, furthest away from an official-looking man sitting at a wooden desk.

"What's happening?" Percy asked Peter.

"More trains. More men. I think I'll take a little wander, see who's in charge of all the horses."

A cat always trusts his sixth sense, and all of the fur on the back of Peter's neck was standing on end. The tension in the air caught on the rough surface of his tongue. He sensed vibrations, like excitement, but darker. Something was up.

Tearful men in uniform clung to their horses, stroking them, talking tenderly, as if they would never see them again. But other men wearing a different uniform, white shirts, long white aprons with a stained kerchief hanging down, had gathered around the man sitting at his wooden desk. Peter couldn't work out who these strangers were. Some of them clasped a wodge of money in their fist as they started moving along the line of horses, but all of them were eager-eyed, scrutinising the horses with great interest.

Peter moved closer to a soldier who was talking fondly to his horse.

"I'm sorry boy. I don't know what to do. You kept me alive - and now this. I never thought the day would come," he said. But one of the men in aprons moved him aside and led his horse away.

The stranger paid some money to the man sitting at the wooden desk, then set off through the streets. Peter followed, keeping pace through every twist and turn. When the man with the apron stopped in front of a shop, Peter watched as he led the horse down an alleyway to the back of the building. Not much was displayed in the shop window, but Peter recognised enough to know what would be sold there.

"No! No!" he meowed. How could they do such a thing? He ran hard, panting, finding it difficult to catch each breath. By the time he reached Percy, a quarter of the horses had already been led away from the line. Men in aprons steadily untied the reins, walked more horses away.

Percy's nostrils flared. "There's something going on. I don't like it," he said.

"I know. I know. I'm thinking."

"Forget what Private Bainbridge said about us sticking together. I don't think that's going to work," said Percy. "You can go home Peter. Just jump on the train and go home. I'll be all right."

There was no way he could smuggle Percy onto the train without Private Bainbridge to help him. But Percy was right, no-one would notice a cat squeezing between their feet. After a little train ride, and a sail across the seas, he'd be home, back on his rock, listening to the skylarks singing.

Peter checked the line. Half the horses had disappeared now. "Well, my friend, it's been quite an adventure after all, just like you said it would be. Don't worry, Percy. Everything will be all right," Peter said.

Percy smiled, whinnied a bit, and while his eyes were fixed on the men in aprons edging towards him, Peter ran off and boarded the nearest train. It was very crowded, so he had to be careful not to be stomped on by a pair of boots. Some of the carriages had men sitting at a table playing cards, with other men crowding round watching, waiting for the train to set off. Peter had seen men playing these sort of card games before. They involved money, frayed tempers, winners and losers. The games didn't always end well.

Peter put on his friendliest smile and leapt up onto the table to join them.

"Look! It's a one-eyed cat," one man said. The men all laughed, so Peter meowed, made himself comfy.

Before boarding the train he'd noticed a few interesting things: the official-looking man sitting at his wooden desk was handing out official-looking pieces of paper to the men. The men took this official-looking bit of paper because they had to show it to a guard before he would allow them to board the train. After that the men carefully folded up their bit of paper, put it in their pocket, and climbed aboard.

It was a long shot, but it was the only plan he had. A one-eyed cat might have a fit. While he was having a fit, he might scatter the pack of cards, causing all of the men to leap about, desperate to retrieve their winning hand. While they were leaping about a clever one-eyed cat might use his teeth, and the odd claw, to retrieve an official-looking piece of paper from a man's pocket.

And that's exactly what Peter did. Five minutes later, with the piece of paper clenched between his teeth, he ran over to Percy.

"Peter! What are you doing here? I thought you'd gone."

"And leave you here alone? Are you mad?" Peter was finding it hard to talk at the same time as holding a piece of paper. "Here! Take hold of this in your teeth, and don't drop it!" he said.

Fortunately, the man who'd tied Percy to the fence hadn't done a very good job, so it didn't take Peter long to untie the reins.

"Come on," he said, "Give me back that bit of paper. We're getting on that train."

The guard looked surprised, but the look in his eye filled Peter with hope. Both cat and horse had dribbled on the piece of paper, but the man didn't seem to mind. He wiped off the dribble with his sleeve and then gave the document his full attention.

"I see," he said. "It appears that this piece of paper allows one soldier to board my train."

Peter nudged Percy forwards. Percy whinnied.

"I take it that the soldier in question is this brave horse. Well, you look like one of the finest soldiers I've every laid eyes on. And your paperwork is in order: so you may board my train. We'd best hurry. The train is about to leave."

As the guard took hold of the reins and led Percy to the last carriage, with his sixth sense on the look out for trouble, Peter trotted a little way behind in case something went wrong. Some men gave the guard a funny look, but the guard paid them no attention.

All the doors slammed, BANG! BANG! BANG! The train hooted, and its great wheels started turning. Peter kept pace with the slow moving train and the one door that was still open. But the guard was standing in his way, blocking his chance to leap aboard. Without an official-looking bit of paper it seemed that the man had no intention of letting Peter jump on. But Percy was safe. That's all that mattered. Peter would just have to find his own way home.

"Come on soldier! You'll have to run faster than that!" shouted the guard. "Yes, you! You clever cat. Hop on board or you'll miss the train!"

With that he scooped Peter up in his big hand and plonked him next to Percy's warm and welcoming nose.

CHAPTER 12

Nearly But Not Quite

AFTER THE LONG TRAIN RIDE, boarding the ship was easy. With so many people pushing and shoving, and several other horses that had escaped the butcher's knife to mingle with, Peter and Percy made it safely on board without anyone trying to stop them.

The weather, as if determined to cause a shipwreck, took a turn for the worse not long after they left Calais harbour. Inky black seas rose as high as the tallest mountains Peter had ever seen, with great waves whooshing into the air and crashing down on them with a terrible growl. The wind, like the brother of the angry seas, howled and yelled in harmony, scaring both cat and horse half to death. They braced themselves, waiting for the ship to snap in half, or for the sea to crash in and drown them. But after three tempestuous days at last the sun showed his happy face. From then on the ship sailed through sweet and contented waters to bring them safely, all the way home.

Or nearly home, back to Southampton, the place where they'd started their journey.

"Soon we'll see Harold," Percy said.

Peter hoped so. But he'd heard the soldiers talking. They feared the Spanish flu. Too many men had died of it, more than in the fighting they said, and Harold had been so ill. But Peter decided not to say anything to Percy. Why worry him while there was still hope that they would find Harold, happy and well, safely at home?

So instead, with a wink and a snigger, he said, "Are we there yet?"

CHAPTER 13

The Last Hiccup

IN ANOTHER OF THOSE DAWN MORNINGS filled with an eerie grey light, they arrived at Southampton. But however tired the men felt, the grey skies and the dim light could do nothing to dampen their spirits. They smiled and cheered as they disembarked, happy to be alive and very grateful to be home. Peter felt the same way, elated, a grinning cat that had got the cream. When he watched the horses being winched off the ship, he held his breath a bit. Percy was right - it did look unnatural to see a horse hanging in the air, swaying like a strange wingless bird caught in a breeze. Relieved to be a cat, Peter tiptoed down the gangplank, careful to avoid being crushed by the mass of heavy boots of men in a hurry to reach home and their loved ones.

Soon he and Percy would be home too. As he'd already been safely winched off the ship, Peter wondered why Percy was taking so long, and went to look for him. He found him, together with the other horses, tied up to a metal barrier. Peter's ears flattened against his head. With all the horses standing in a line, a group of men appeared out of nowhere. They gathered around the dejected horses like a swarm of flies. The sight looked horribly familiar.

Percy snorted, gave a whinny of fear. He knew what they were up to all right. Peter darted back and forth, trying to think what to do. This time there was no piece of paper to snatch allowing Percy to be set free. There was no friendly guard, no Private Bainbridge, no Harold. Peter's heart missed a beat. They'd made it this far only for Percy to be sold off. He couldn't let that happen. But what could a cat do? He licked his lips. His mouth felt as dry as old bones in a butcher's window. When Percy whinnied again Peter climbed up onto his friend's back.

"It'll be all right, Percy. Wherever you go, I go, you know that," he said, trying to comfort his friend.

"Not this time, Peter. I can smell blood. I can smell it on those men's hands. Just like the last time. They're butchers looking for meat."

Peter thought of his rock, of Blagdon and all the familiar sights that he loved. But he realised that home would only feel like home if he could see Percy, galloping across the beautiful green fields, with his long chestnut tail dancing in the breeze.

"They're not laying a finger on you," he growled. But if he meant to stop them he needed to think of something, and be quick about it.

From up on Percy's back Peter scanned the crowd. He could see a man wearing a suit patterned with so many squares and lines that it made Peter's eyes jump. This man was talking to the butchers as they shuffled along the line of horses. But then more men, broader shouldered with ruddy cheeks, joined in, probing and pinching flesh to find the best animal.

Peter widened his gaze, and caught sight of a tall man heading north, moving at a leisurely pace as he made his way through the crowds.

"Wait here," Peter said to Percy.

"I'm tied up! What else can I do?" Percy moaned.

"Yes. Yes."

Peter lifted his tail high. Holding a northerly direction he wove his way through a perilous cluster of marching feet. From time to time he looked up, checking faces, until at last he reached the one he was after. Weaving his spine between the man's legs, he vigorously rubbed himself against them.

"What the …!" Lieutenant Richard Tolson bent down. "Well if it isn't Peter-the-Rock! How on earth did you get here?"

There was no way to tell him, and no time to waste in idle conversation. Peter had discovered as a kitten that men don't like being bitten by a cat, so being careful not to bite into flesh, he sank his teeth into the thick material of the Lieutenant's trouser leg. Once he had a firm grip he pulled with all his might.

"Steady on, Peter!"

Peter tugged again. If he had to, he'd drag the man one step at a time to where Percy waited. After three more tugs Richard yanked his leg free and Peter's heart sank. But instead of marching away, the Lieutenant leant down and patted Peter on the head.

"I get it! You want me to follow you. I've no idea why, but Harold told me that you are a very clever cat. So we can do this without you drilling any more holes in my trousers! You lead Peter-the-Rock, and I'll follow."

After that they moved swiftly. The Lieutenant was quick-witted. He grasped the true nature of the problem as soon as he saw Percy tied up with the other horses.

"Excuse me! What's your name?" he said to the bossy looking man in the gaudy suit.

"My name is Cyril. Are you another farmer wanting to buy?"

"Do I look like a farmer? Now see here, Cyril, I think there's been a terrible mistake. You're surely not intending to sell this horse for meat!" Richard said, gesturing at Percy.

"Meat, or to work on a farm. It makes no difference to me. I've just got to clear the lot of them out of the way."

"Well you can't sell this horse!" Richard said.

"Er ... well, I can!" Cyril replied, wobbling his head from side to side and widening his eyes so that he looked like a frog.

"This horse belongs to an officer," Richard said, gesturing at Percy again.

"So you say, but who's to say you're right. To me it looks just like any other horse."

Peter reckoned Richard might need some help. Percy belonged to an officer, all right, and he had letters engraved on his hoof to prove it. Rapid meowing, and dramatic circling of Percy's leg, attracted Richard's attention.

"What? Oh, yes, that's right! Well done, Peter. Look here, Cyril. You see these initials engraved on this horse's hoof?"

Cyril peered, grunted a bit, shrugged.

"HBR. They stand for Harold Burge Robson, the rightful owner of this horse."

"That's nothing to do with me. My job is to sell all of these horses, and you're getting in my way!" he said, jabbing his index finger at Richard's face.

"This can't be right!" Richard said. "I thought only the French ate their horses."

"Times have changed. Now we're all starving we'll eat whatever we can afford to put on our plate. Horse, rabbit, donkey, dog. It's all better than watching your children starve to death. So if you want this flea-ridden bag of bones you'll have to buy it. Them's the rules of this 'ere game."

Lieutenant Tolson took a deep breath. The look in his eye was enough to hold Cyril's attention. "Now you listen to me, you've got a job to do, and I understand that. This horse might be tired and weary, but he's worth his weight in gold."

But a stocky man, with hands as huge as carpet beaters and ears to match, shuffled closer, his big ears drinking in every word that Richard said. Peter didn't like the look of him. The man sidled across, licked his lips, patted Percy all over, lifted his tail. He didn't seem to know much about horses, because trying to force a stallion's mouth open is a bad idea. Percy snapped at him then stamped his front feet, forcing the man to leap out of the way to avoid his toes being crushed.

"Er …." Richard glanced at the man, then back at Cyril. "This horse, his name is Percy, and he saved Harold's life many times during this terrible war, together with this cat, Peter-the-rock. They may look like a cat and a horse to you, but Peter and Percy are war heroes. Do you hear me? War heroes! So you show some respect."

Cyril backed a safe distance away before he dared to open his mouth to speak again, "War heroes are two-a-penny now the war's over, mate," he yelled and flapped his arms about. "Now, if you don't mind, I need to get these horses sold. So, like I say, you want to save this horse from being a chop on someone's dinner plate, Mr Mighty Officer Sir, you'll have to put your money where your mouth is."

"I'll buy this horse!" the stocky man said.

Richard shook his head. "That horse isn't for sale!" he said.

"Oh yes he is!" snapped Cyril.

"Oh no he isn't!" Richard said.

"Oh yes he bloomin' well is," barked Cyril.

"Good!" said the man with huge hands, "Because I need a horse to pull my plough. The other one dropped dead on me. It's tough work. This one looks like the best you've got. The others look like they'd drop dead in a week. So I'll take him off your hands. I'm a busy man, so let's not mess about. I'll give you above the going rate to seal the deal.

Forty-five pounds - job done!"

At this point it became clear to Peter that the wodge of cash that the Lieutenant had pulled out of his pocket looked very thin compared to the farmer's pile of notes. But Richard said "Fifty pounds!" quickly, and shoved his money back in his pocket.

The farmer smiled like a fox who knew where all the chickens were hiding. "Sixty!" he said.

Richard straightened his spine. "Sixty-five! This horse belongs to Harold Burge Robson, a very brave officer, and I'm taking him home."

"Even a posh officer needs to eat, so you can tell your fancy friend that unless I have a good horse to plough my fields, your Harold will be having to eat his silver cutlery! I may be just a farmer to you, but I think you'll find I'm the sort of man who doesn't give up until the job is done! Seventy pounds!" he barked, flicking through his wodge of money.

Cyril's head swung back and forth on his skinny neck as the two men bartered for Percy's life. But it was no good, Richard tried to look as if he had all the money in the world, but Peter knew they were reaching the end of the road.

"Seventy-five pounds," Richard said through gritted teeth.

"Eighty pounds!" the farmer's smile grew wider as if he knew this would be the winning number.

"Right. Right," the Lieutenant said, kicking at the dirt with the toe of his boot.

They were all out of luck. Percy would end his life being worked to death pulling a plough. Peter couldn't bare to think of it.

"Be ready to kick him, stamp on him. Distract him while I try to untie you!" Peter said.

"It's no good, Peter. I'm done for. I was lucky to make it this far! Lots of horses died on the battlefield. You go back to your rock. Go home and leave me here," Percy whinnied.

Leaping up onto his friend's back, Peter spread his feet wide, arched his back and bared his teeth. "I'll have that farmer's eye out before I'll let him take you away, Percy!"

"Are we done?" Cyril turned to Richard, who was watching the grinning farmer counting out his money.

"I …," Richard stammered. "Actually, no. You said that I need to put my money where my mouth is, so that's exactly what I'm going to do. Here's my watch. I think you'll find it's worth a good deal more than eighty pounds."

"What good is a pile of nickel to me, mate?" Cyril asked.

"Cyril, you will remember that I told you Percy is worth his weight in gold. This watch was given to me by my father. It might not equal him weight for weight, but just like Percy, it is made out of solid gold."

The farmer's cheeks flushed crimson. He puffed them out, crushed his money into a ball with his sweaty hands.

Richard untied Percy. "Come on you two. We've got half an hour before our train arrives. Just enough time to send Harold a telegram."

HAROLD MEET ME AT THE RIDLEY PLACE WITH JASPER
DAY AFTER TOMORROW stop
BE READY TO CELEBRATE stop
YOU WON'T BELIEVE WHAT I'M BRINGING HOME stop

CHAPTER 14

The Last Mile

LIEUTENANT RICHARD TOLSON NO LONGER HAD a gold watch, but luckily he still had his cash in his pocket, enough to buy a horse and a cat a comfy place on the train from Southampton to London Waterloo, together with some food. They all ate slowly, savouring each mouthful.

"We're going home," Percy said while munching on a mouthful of hay.

"Are we there yet?" Peter replied. "Ha! Ha! Ha!" He couldn't keep his tail from flicking back and forth with excitement. This time they really were going home. Nothing could stop them now.

Before the war against the Germans had turned the world upside down, it might not have been a very familiar sight, to see a man *and* a cat riding on a horse through the streets of London. But it would be a long time before people regained a sense of what 'normal' looked like. So as Lieutenant Tolson, Percy and Peter made their way from Waterloo to Kings Cross Station to catch their final train home, no one so much as glanced in their direction.

Richard paid for more tickets and they set off on the last part of their journey.

"What're you thinking?" Percy said.

"About my rock," Peter said. But really he'd been thinking about Archie-the-Fiend. By now he would have claimed Peter's rock as his own, taken over the fields and the trees. Peter shuddered, remembering how afraid Archie had made him feel. But that was when he'd been a cat named Ridley. Now he was Peter-the-Rock. He must remember that.

In the early afternoon, with the rays of sunlight still sparkling through the ever-green trees, they reached the South Gate of Blagdon Hall. The stone bulls, white and unblemished, sat on their plinths on either side of the gateway. As they'd always done, the one on the left faced them in greeting, while the one on the right faced away, looking longingly towards the house.

Percy snorted, flicked his tail and leapt into the air.

"Steady boy! Nearly there!" Richard said.

After a few twists and turns, Blagdon Hall came into view. A woman dressed in black, with a white apron saw them. She waved, yelled something, then raced into the house. A man came running out then, saw them and hurled his cap in the air.

"That's Private Bainbridge!" said Peter.

After that there was more yelling. A tall man came rushing outside, followed by a flood of people who came flowing out of the door behind him.

Percy sniffed the air. After one jolting stride, which nearly threw Peter off, the stallion broke into a gallop.

"Easy now, Percy!" Richard laughed.

But Peter knew there would be no stopping Percy now: he'd seen Harold. Richard let go of the reins with one hand, and grabbed hold of Peter just in time, because he was about to be flung off Percy's back all together.

"I don't believe my eyes!" they could hear Harold shouting, as he came running towards them. "Richard! Richard! You found them both!" he said, reaching up to shake Richard's hand. "I can never thank you enough. However did you do it?"

"It was Peter's doing, not mine," said Richard. "Peter found me, not the other way round. After that he didn't give up until he'd made me understand that Percy was in serious trouble. You're right, he's a very brave and clever cat!"

"My boys, my heroes! I thought I'd never see either of you again, and yet here you are. Percy! Percy!" Lost for words Harold nuzzled against Percy's cheek. "And you, Peter-the-Rock, what a brave cat you've been," he said, tickling Peter behind the ear, "And lucky! Because who would believe it! Look at us! We all came safely home. It's nothing short of a miracle. But, I mustn't forget, there's two very important people I think you'd like to meet."

They all looked to where he was pointing.

"Well I never! Do you see them Percy and Peter? It's only King George and Queen Mary. I reckon this is the finest welcome home a horse and a cat have ever had!" said Richard.

After much talking and laughing and patting of Percy, they all settled down in the grand drawing room, with Peter being the last to stroll through the door. At which point he saw Obadiah Blackhart striding across the room and heading straight for him. Peter readied himself, bared his teeth.

"No! No! That won't be necessary," Obadiah Blackhart said. "I apologise, unreservedly. I mistook you for a flea-infested, worm-riddled feline. I see now that I was very wrong. You, Peter-the-Rock, are the finest of cats."

With that the butler placed a silver dish on the floor at Peter's feet. Peter sniffed it, wary. But it turned out to be a bowl of the finest meat, finely chopped and covered in gravy. Peter had never smelt anything so delicious.

"From now on," the butler said, "I shall be making sure, personally, that you are treated in the manner that you deserve."

After Peter had eaten all of the tasty meat, Queen Mary took a shine to him. She placed him on her knee, and gave him some tasty treats, biscuits and cheese and all that he could eat. With his belly satisfyingly full for the first time in years, Peter's tail began to twitch. He really wanted to see his rock again. So while everyone was busy raising glasses and celebrating, he sneaked out through an open window and headed off to the field.

The sun, already dipping his head, spread a lovely warm glow across the rock. Peter stopped. He'd noticed a shadowy shape slinking back and forth, predatory, hostile.

"Hello Archie," Peter said. "Nice of you to keep my rock warm while I've been away."

"Huh?" Archie swung round, claws sharp, ready for a fight. "This is my rock now!" he hissed.

"No, it isn't." Peter sat down, cleaned his whiskers, smiled. "I know you want to fight me. You're thinking, it'll be easy because you beat me last time. But you look like you've put on weight. It's all that sitting about on my rock. And I'd better warn you, while I've been away I've learnt a lot about fighting. I've survived gunfire, explosions, starvation.

I've killed rats bigger than you. Actually I've eaten rats that are bigger than you. Several of them," Peter said, licking his lips and circling his rock. "This is my home, Archie, and I love it. This is my rock, and I don't like the way you're wiping your furry bum on it!"

Before Archie had time to move, Peter leapt at him, and knocked the Fiend to the ground with one strike of his muscular front paw. Archie-the-Fiend let out a yelp, and then ran.

Peter strolled back and forth on his rock, familiarising himself with his home. The lingering stench of Archie-the-Fiend would wash away with the next good shower of rain. As the long shadows of evening fell, Peter studied his outline. His physique looked a little on the thin side, but muscular, feline. Tomorrow morning life would return to normal. He would watch Percy galloping across the field, his tail flicking away the flies. The skylarks would sing overhead and, without fear, Peter-the-Rock would go hunting for his breakfast. Contented, Peter settled down to give himself a good clean up.

"Harold was right," Peter said to a passing hedgehog, "it is amazing the courage you can find when you're fighting to save your home and the ones you love!"

Letting out a long purr of satisfaction, Peter gazed into the distance and glimpsed a flicker of tail as Archie-the-Fiend ran, as fast as his dumpy legs could carry him, out through the South Gates of Blagdon Hall, an enemy conquered, crushed and never to be seen again.

The End

This was a

DizzyB

Production

Lightning Source UK Ltd.
Milton Keynes UK
UKHW02f1922201018
330903UK00001B/2/P